Mr. Mohamed was born in Tanzania. After graduation from high school, he went to Moscow in the Soviet Union to complete his university education. His first novel about his personal life in Moscow during the peak Communist era was published in 1975. After about forty years, Mr. Mohamed has penned his second book—not about his personal life but about the meaning of life in general.

He lives in Calgary, Alberta, Canada.

I would like to dedicate this book to my friend, JinLan Chen, who not only provided motivation and inspiration in creating this story but also supported me all the way to the end.

H. E. Mohamed

MEILI

AUSTIN MACAULEY PUBLISHERS™

LONDON • CAMBRIDGE • NEW YORK • SHARJAH

Copyright © H. E. Mohamed (2019)

Ordering Information:
Quantity sales: special discounts are available on quantity purchases by corporations, associations, and others. For details, contact the publisher at the address below.

Publisher's Cataloging-in-Publication data
Mohamed, H. E.
Meili

ISBN 9781643786018 (Paperback)
ISBN 9781643786025 (Hardback)
ISBN 9781645368304 (ePub e-book)

The main category of the book — YOUNG ADULT FICTION / Social Themes / Religion & Faith

Library of Congress Control Number: 2019908520

www.austinmacauley.com/us

First Published (2019)
Austin Macauley Publishers LLC
40 Wall Street, 28th Floor
New York, NY 10005
USA

mail-usa@austinmacauley.com
+1 (646) 5125767

My sincere thanks to Hanif Mohamed, whose nagging and pestering started this mission.

Prologue

She was 11 years old when I first met her—very quiet, shy, and reserved. She did not talk at all, though she spoke English very well, not to mention her mother tongue.

To date, I still wonder if my meeting her was 'written'; was it to be or just a stroke of luck?

Sometimes, I sit on the balcony and try to figure out if God really works in mysterious ways or is it just God's weird sense of humor that humans have difficulty understanding?

Chapter 1

It was a snowy, cold November day when I got a phone call from my girlfriend of six years.

"It's over," she said.

"What's over?" I asked, a little confused.

"Our relationship, I am through," she politely replied.

"What?!" I exclaimed, more shocked than confused. "What happened? Did I do something to deserve this news?" I could barely talk.

"No, no, it's not you," she said, "you are a good person. It's me—I just don't stay with a man for too long, although you have been an exception, sorry," and the phone went dead in my ears.

I could feel every brick of my future home come tumbling down on my head, windows shattering, doors ripping apart, and my dreams? 'What dreams?' I asked myself later on.

There is no justice, how could a person you have known, trusted, and cared for six years do this to you? No reason, no nothing!

I called her back, three times that day, but the phone was not answered. I went to her house—nobody was home, so I left her keys in the mailbox and walked back to my car disappointed, sad, and totally heartbroken. A dried-up apple tree in front of her house, just a few months ago had had hundreds of little red apples on it, stared at me and somehow I felt that the tree was telling me, 'Do not despair, my friend, time heals everything. Look at me, I am all dried up now but wait until spring, and I shall have fresh new leaves.'

As I sat in my car, it occurred to me that somebody once said, "Everything happens for a reason."

Chapter 2

Meet Luigi. He is my friend and I call him Lou. He is very close to me but sometimes I don't see him for weeks.

It was Saturday, three weeks after I broke up with Julie (that's my ex-girlfriend's name), when Lou called.

"Hi, Arif, what's up?" Same old Lou. Always 'what's up?'

"Nothing. How you doing? Long time no hear," I said.

"Are you up for some wings and beer?" he asked.

"Sure, why not?"

"Will Julie come too?"

"No, I'll see you around 6 o'clock? Same place?" I asked.

"Yeah, same place. 6 o'clock."

There is this sports bar in town that Julie and I used to go for chicken wings and beer every Wednesday before we went to play bridge (card game) at the club. Lou would join us there some Wednesdays when he wasn't working late.

Lou was already seated in a booth at the bar when I got there a few minutes after six. We exchanged greetings and ordered our food when the waitress came by.

An hour later, we had finished eating, and I told him about Julie and me breaking up. Lou politely said nothing, just kept looking at me, probably not believing what I was saying.

"Don't just sit there and stare at me. Say something," I said, getting a little irritated.

"What do you want me to say?" he said, "I am sorry."

"Thank you, but it is now in the past."

"Okay," he said, "so, let's go out someplace and have fun."

"Where?" I asked. "We are already out here."

He chuckled, "Not here, this is not out. Let's go to a movie or maybe a night club."

"What movie is playing, do you know?" I asked.

"Well, there is this new Twilight saga movie called 'New Moon' just released. Let's go watch it."

"Are you kidding? I am not watching a Twilight movie."

He looked at me like I was some kind of crazy guy because I remember he liked the first Twilight movie although I didn't.

He finally gulped down his beer and said, "Okay, let's go someplace else then."

"Where? No night clubs, I am too old for that."

"How about we go to the casino, we can have a drink there, play some blackjack or slot machines and just hang out."

I thought for a little while and then said, "Casino might be alright, I haven't gone to the casino for a long time." At least hanging out with Lou would be much better than sitting home in my lonely apartment.

An hour later, Lou and I walked into the NE Casino off Barlow Trail. The place was busy, people shouting at the tables, machines jingling, and you could hear loud music playing from the live band.

We walked around, looking at all the action and then, suddenly, I stopped at the craps table. Not that there was anything unusual about craps, it was the sight of one dealer that attracted my attention. There were ten players at the table, six on one side, and four on the other side. A craps table has a box man sitting on one side in the middle of the table with one dealer on either side and a stick man across the box man who handles the dice and all the central bets. Players all stand on the stick man's side facing the dealers who handle all the chips. I didn't have a clue how the game was played. One player was throwing the dice. I just watched as the chips went back and forth from the dealer to the players and vice versa as players kept betting on the numbers.

The dealer that made me pause there was a young Asian woman. I strained my eyes to read her name on the nametag pinned to her shirt. 'ShuYa,' it read. ShuYa was about 5 feet four inches tall, slender figure from what I could see, beautiful features; high cheekbones, narrow dark eyes, high forehead, and long black hair parted in the middle so it fell in front covering both her cheeks. I stood there at the side of the table and watched her efficiently handling chips, a pleasant smile on her face as she worked like a professional dealer.

"Let's move, man," I heard Lou's distant voice, sounded distant although Lou was standing right beside me. I must have been totally mesmerized by ShuYa, I could not take my eyes off her beautiful face.

"Hey," Lou nudged me. "I am going to the bar for a beer," he said and started walking away.

I stood there looking at ShuYa for about fifteen minutes when a new dealer showed up and everybody shifted around except the box man who must be the pit boss. ShuYa walked off the table, down the hallway, and through the door into the 'staff only' area. Must be her break, I figured as I watched her swiftly walk by me. Strange thoughts went through my mind; was she single, married, kids, had a husband, parents? Who was she? Was there any way I could find out?

Six years I had been with one woman and three weeks after we broke up, I got attracted to another woman. It felt strange that all this time I didn't look around, never noticed another woman. I must have been totally blind or must have been happy with what I had although that happiness disintegrated like a burning wooden block.

That night at home, I searched the Internet for casino games, found 'craps' and studied it. Tough game, but all I needed was the basics. Next day, I went back to the casino to look for ShuYa. No luck, she wasn't there. I looked through the whole casino, every table game, but ShuYa was not to be found. Maybe she worked the earlier shift. Disappointed, I went home.

Every day for the rest of the week, I visited the casino to look for ShuYa but didn't see her. Was it my luck or maybe it was not to be, I thought later on. Was ShuYa real or was she a figment of my imagination? Was I going crazy thinking about her?

Come Saturday, a week had gone by when walking into the casino, I decided that if ShuYa wasn't there, then I might as well forget about her. At least during the week I learned to play craps. To my surprise and joy, ShuYa was at the craps table. I ran and joined other players at the table, full of energy and enthusiasm. The whole time I was at the table, joking, laughing, and having fun, I kept my eyes on ShuYa. To me, her beauty was unimaginable. Was she that beautiful? I suppose 'beauty is in the eye of the beholder.'

Later that night, I had a little chat with the pit boss during the break who informed me that ShuYa only worked at the casino on the weekends, mostly on Saturdays and sometimes on Fridays if the casino had a shortage of dealers. This became my escapade for the weekend. Two weeks later, I managed to talk to ShuYa and invited her for dinner. At first she was hesitant but asked me for my phone number and said she would call. Actually, she didn't call me for a month; Christmas and New Year went by, although I saw her every week at her work. I figured due to the holidays she was probably busy, so I did not raise the dinner issue.

It was Saturday afternoon, mid-January, when I finally got a call from ShuYa.

"Hi, Arif," she said, "do you still want to take me out for dinner?"

Bit surprised that she finally called, I said, "Yes, of course, I wouldn't have asked you if I did not want to."

"I am off next Saturday, how about then?" she asked.

Bursting with joy, I said happily, "Sure, next Saturday sounds excellent. Give me your address and the time and I'll pick you up."

"Okay, I will let you know." She hung up.

Did she really mean that or maybe she was just pulling my leg, probably sitting around with friends and laughing, having fun. A mere assumption, but I really hoped that was not the case. That night I went to the casino, saw ShuYa at the craps table but did not talk to her. She acted the usual, polite and friendly to all the players including me.

At noon, the next Saturday, I got a call from ShuYa.

"Hi, Arif, how are you?" she asked, as soon as I picked up the phone.

"I am fine, thank you, and you?" I replied, knowing that she was true to her word.

"Are we still going out tonight?"

"Of course, what time?" I asked.

"Would seven o'clock work? I have to let my daughter's baby-sitter know."

For a minute or two I hesitated, totally surprised that she had a little girl. "How old is your daughter?" I finally asked.

"You surprised? Does it bother you?" She must have sensed my hesitation.

"Surprised, yes; bothered, no," I said, hoping not to offend her. "So how old is she?"

"She is eleven."

"Tell you what. Forget the baby-sitter and bring her along. We will go to a family restaurant," I said, "it would be nice to meet her."

"That is very kind of you. Are you sure?"

"Yes, I am sure, bring her with you, and let's make it six o'clock."

That settled, she gave me her address and phone number to call her when I got there as she lived in an apartment building.

The night was cold when I got to her place at exactly six o'clock. I didn't have to phone her as she was already in the lobby of the apartment building. As soon as I got out of the car, she stepped outside, followed by a little girl all bundled up in a long winter coat. ShuYa walked towards me, said hello, gave me a hug, and said, "This is my daughter," pointing at a little girl following her, barely three feet tall and quite thin. I moved closer to the little girl who just stood there looking at me. Small, round face, dark eyes, and long black hair parted in the middle dropping down along her cheeks, just like her mother.

I bent down to face her and said, "Hi, I am Arif, what is your name?"

"Meili," the little girl responded very quietly.

"Nice meeting you, Meili, how old are you?" I asked.

"Eleven."

That was all she said to me the entire evening, but that evening was the turning point of my life.

Chapter 3

Almost three years went by, ShuYa and I got closer as the time kept moving faster. ShuYa, besides being so beautiful, was a very kind and caring person. She had just finished her accounting degree by taking courses in the evening while working full time at her job with an oil related company, working weekends at the casino, and taking care of her daughter Meili and me! All at the same time and never once complained. It amazed me how much energy she had.

During the early days of my relationship with ShuYa, Meili hardly talked to me. She was certainly jealous—I felt—that her mother was paying more attention to me than her, though that was not the case. ShuYa cared for Meili, always worrying about her schooling, her health, and her well-being. Meili, on the other hand, did not realize this and it seemed to me that she did not like me. She kept herself busy reading books or playing video games and never involved herself in any conversation with me or anybody else. I once asked ShuYa if Meili was feeling okay. "She is fine, she just doesn't talk when you are around," said ShuYa, "she likes to read."

As time passed, Meili loosened up and slowly started to talk to me and got involved in our conversations more instead of either sitting on the couch reading or staying in her room. I figured as she matured, she more or less started to understand life because she spent lots of time on computer and internet.

It was Saturday night that December, just a week before Christmas (ShuYa had quit working at the casino) that Meili came and sat beside me on the sofa and asked, "Hey, Arif, tell me what is LOVE? How do you define love and what does it mean?"

"Don't you know what love means?" I asked gently as ShuYa ran over from the kitchen and sat down beside us.

"I don't," said ShuYa, "so tell us."

"Yeah, how do you explain love?" Meili asked. "Everybody says 'I love you' or love this or that, so what does love really mean?"

"Love means never having to say you're sorry," I said smartly.

"No!" Meili screamed, banging her fist on the sofa, "that is such bullshit. I have come across that before. It is from an old movie."

ShuYa laughed, got up, and walked back to the kitchen, muttering something about dinner getting overcooked.

"Alright, so you don't buy that," I said, shifting my position sideways to face her, "actually this phrase comes from Erich Segal's novel *Love Story* and has been quoted in a movie and many TV series, but do you know that word 'love' is one of the most commonly used words in English language and probably in other languages also. There are many definitions of love and I am sure you must have checked them out on the internet and dictionary. So, the question is, why are you asking me to explain love. To bug

20

me? To make fun of me? Or to find out if I am good enough to answer your query."

Meili smiled, looked me straight in the eye, and said, "No, it is not true. I am not trying to harass you. I seriously want to know what you think love really means. Internet has got like tons of different versions or explanations of love and that does not really make sense."

I sat there, shocked, didn't have a clue what was going on and why me? Did she really think I was smart enough to explain love to her? I am not a philosopher. Her mother, ShuYa, has a degree in philosophy, why can't she ask her?

As if she read my mind, Meili said, "My mom wants to know your definition of love, she is not sure what exactly love means."

"Now hold on a second," I protested, "that is not fair. She wants to know my definition of love? I thought you were the one who wanted to know what love means."

"I do, but my mom could not explain properly, so she asked me to ask you," Meili said with a smile on her face.

Just as I was about to give in, ShuYa called from the kitchen to set up the table. Dinner was ready.

"Okay, let's go eat first and then we shall continue this topic."

After we had a hearty meal, cleaned up the table and dishes, Meili grabbed my hand and pulled me to the living room saying, "Can we continue with our talk?"

We made ourselves comfortable on sofa, ShuYa brought the coffee, and I began, "Like I said before, the word love is used in many ways, for example, 'I love my cat' or 'he loves playing music' and so on. This is only a more emphasized version of 'like.' For example, you could say 'he likes playing music,' except when the word love is put in there, it is just a step ahead of like. Real meaning of love and this is my version is 'strong affection for another person' which includes caring, forgiving, helping, unselfishness, kindness, politeness, and generosity."

"Wow! All that?" Meili exclaimed.

"Yes, all that and then some," I replied, "love arises from blood ties for example parents love their children and vice versa, everybody loves their siblings. And then love for another person like between a man and woman arises from admiration, warm attachment, concern for the good of another etc."

"So, when you say you love somebody, does it mean that you are prepared to do all that caring and forgiving and all that mumbo jumbo?" Meili asked with a smirk on her face.

"No, the word is not 'prepared.' The feeling comes natural and if both parties love each other, then all that mumbo jumbo, as you called it, comes naturally and life becomes a very wonderful thing."

"In short, you become a slave to another person," Meili said.

"Caring and doing things for another person does not mean you are his/her slave. If both parties love each other, then their actions and words they utter are controlled. They try not to hurt each other and if unintentionally one does something that might hurt the other, then that other will understand and forgive," I tried to explain. "Remember that phrase 'love means never having to say you are sorry.' The way I look at it is if your actions do not hurt the other, then you have nothing to apologize for. Thus the word 'sorry' does not exist."

Both mother and daughter sat there looking at me for a few minutes, probably perplexed or amazed, I could not tell, then finally ShuYa joked, "Since when you became Socrates?"

"Hey, Socrates was a great philosopher," I said. "Don't insult the great man by comparing him to me. And by the way, Socrates as far as I know did not say anything about love. He had different views of gods recognized by the then city people, while my view on love is simple and probably agreed upon by most of the people of our time."

"You sound offended," ShuYa said politely, "I was only kidding, I could have said Confucius, but Socrates was the first name that came to my mind."

"No, I am not offended, not to worry—"

"That's it?!" Meili interrupted. "Love comes naturally? I thought first comes the attraction, then the likeness, and then the love."

"So true, but not necessarily. You might be attracted to someone, you might like someone or something, you might even enjoy someone's company, but that doesn't mean that you love that someone," I said. "Love for someone is very special, although many people abuse that word. But then everybody has their own view on love. I gave you my definition of love because that is what you asked me to."

"Words of wisdom," ShuYa said.

"Wisdom cannot be described in words," I said. "Wisdom reveals itself in your actions. Just like love, somebody saying 'I love you' means nothing, anybody can say that, it is the action of that somebody that reveals love."

23

When I came home, I wondered what happened. A sweet, little girl suddenly grew up?

Chapter 4

Six months had passed since Meili inquired about love. She had just finished her elementary school and we were celebrating the occasion when she came back to bug me. It was a hot summer day and we were at my place just about ready to fire up the barbecue when she came out on the balcony and asked, "Arif, you believe in God and religion, don't you?"

"Yes."

"My mom and I don't have any religion, we don't know anything about God," she said. "So, tell us who is God? Where is God? Has anybody seen God? How come people say 'we believe in God'? All the religions talk about God yet nobody knows who God is. How come people believe in something that does not exist? God, it seems, is an illusion. Religions are, as far as I am concerned, designed to scare people by the threat of God's punishment."

Shocked, I listened, trying to figure out how many questions she put forward in the little speech. Could I really explain God and religion to her? And how? I could see that she was maturing, had turned into a beautiful, young teenage girl, but was she that smart to raise intricate questions about God?

ShuYa must have sensed my thoughts. "Meili, Arif is busy right now cooking our meal, can you wait until after dinner?" Phew! I got some time to think about God.

Meili certainly wasn't happy and gave her mom a dirty look. But before ShuYa could say anything, I said, "Strange that you should ask about God because I asked my dad the same question when I was a kid about half a century ago. Only difference is I was not smart or intelligent enough to really find out about God. It was just a kid's curiosity. We will talk about religion and God after supper, okay?"

Two hours later, we were sitting watching TV when Meili again persisted with her query. "So, who is God?"

"God is a word widely used for many different reasons," I said. "You can go on the Internet and check 'Wikipedia' and you'll find multiple pages of different versions of God and all the religious beliefs and explanations of God. I am certainly not an authority on God."

Meili laughed, "I have checked the Wikipedia," she said, "and to be honest, I do not understand most of what it says. You are different, you talk differently and cautiously with your words, and you explain things the way you think is right."

"You flatter me," I said. "How old are you? Fourteen? And you think I am different? Remember one thing, you should never judge others. I try to mind my own business and what others say, think, or do is their business, not mine."

"I think I have noticed that in the last few years, that's why I want to know what you think of religion and God."

"First of all, you have a wrong impression of religion. It is not designed to scare people; on the contrary, religion teaches good things. The word religion actually means 'the pattern of belief and practice' and all religions teach and identify good and bad as perceived by humans. Religion teaches and shows a path to awakening, enlightenment, and eternity. The path to find God." I sounded like a really bad teacher trying to explain religion. "You say your mom and you have no religion, which is also not true."

"Ha, ha," Meili laughed, "we don't have any religion. What religion you think we have? Do you really think that if we believed in any religion, we could find God? If God really exists, then why can't we find him without religion?"

"You didn't get it, did you?" I tried to explain, "Did I not say religion means the pattern of belief and practice? It could be Christianity, Islam, Buddhism, Hinduism or any other or it could be none of the above. It is all about what you believe and practice."

"I don't get it, can you explain that?"

ShuYa, sitting on the recliner chair a little farther from where Meili and I were sitting on the couch, looked at me with an inquisitive look and said, "What exactly does that mean?"

"Alright, listen carefully," I said, like a professor trying to lecture his students, "I'll ask you four questions and all you have to do is answer them truthfully."

"This sounds like fun, are we now going to play games?" Meili asked.

"No games, this is serious. Just four simple questions."

"Okay, let's do it."

"Okay, question number one," I said, "do you ever lie? Or do you always tell the truth?"

"Sometimes," Meili laughed, "when I was little and if I did something wrong, my mom would scream at me and I would lie and say 'I didn't do it.' That would make her madder and she always kept telling me, 'Don't lie. Tell the truth' so, slowly I learned the lesson."

"Good, your mom has taught you well. What you did when you were little is normal, kids usually tend to lie out of fear," I said, "I know your mom doesn't lie or at least she has never lied to me in all these years I have known her. Now, on to question number two: Do you ever take anything that does not belong to you or was not given to you? In short, do you ever steal?"

"No way, my mom would kill me."

"Is that why you would not steal? What if you did not have your mom, would you then take whatever you felt like?"

At this point, ShuYa came to the rescue, "Meili is very honest, she will not touch anything that does not belong to her."

"You agree?" I asked Meili.

"Yeah, why would I take anything that does not belong to me? I am not a thief."

"Very well, that's settled, we now move to question number three: Do you ever do or say anything that would harm or hurt somebody?" I asked.

"Not intentionally, but sometimes I might say something unintentionally that could hurt somebody. Like, the other day, Mary (Meili's childhood friend) and I were playing a video game and I said something and Mary got upset," Meili replied with a sad face, "I really did not mean to hurt her."

"Unintentional mistakes are forgiven, sometimes we all say things that might not go well with others. That is just human nature because we all are different and we all think differently. Main thing is that we try our best not to hurt anybody."

"And now the last question?" ShuYa prompted.

"The last question is tough and more complicated," I said, "it is actually very difficult to answer truthfully."

"Try me," Meili challenged.

"You are actually too young to grasp the real meaning of the question (was I judging her?). I hope as you get older, you will remember what it pertains to."

"Now, now, who is judging who? So, what is the question?" Meili asked.

"This question has three parts," I replied, "first is jealousy or envy, second is greed, and third is pride. Do you get jealous of others' qualities, possessions, or fortune? Are you greedy? Do you always want more? Do you take pride in your achievements and boast about it?"

ShuYa and Meili looked at each other, not saying anything. While I was waiting for their response, I got up and made myself a cup of coffee. Girls did not drink coffee at night, claiming they could not sleep if they drank coffee.

Finally, ShuYa said, "Jealousy is a tough one. Everybody at some point or other feels jealous of others. It is a part of human feelings."

"Well put. But feelings could be controlled. How about greed?"

Meili promptly responded, "I am not greedy."

"That is very good," I said, "you are not greedy, which means you are content with what you have, therefore jealousy goes out the window. How about pride?"

"I feel proud when I get A plus in my school."

"There is nothing wrong in feeling proud of your achievement, as long as you keep it to yourself. What is wrong is boasting about it to others. Having said that," I continued, "we come back to the issue of religion. Every religion preaches all the points we just discussed and more. Thus, you have a religion of your own. You can safely say, 'I don't lie, I don't cheat or steal, I don't hurt anybody, and I am not jealous of others' fortune and THAT is my religion.' If you honestly answered those questions and truthfully believe in what you just said, then you are a good person and you have moved one step closer to finding God."

"What is the second step then?"

I finished my coffee, set the cup down, and said, "Second step is to turn things around. We talked about what you should do. Now comes the issue of what you would do if someone else did the things pertaining to those four questions and it affected you. Because we are surrounded by other human beings, many things will happen more often than you could imagine. So, we go back to question one. What if someone lied to you and you know that it is a lie. How would you take it? Would you tell him on the face that he is a liar, which would, of course, ruin your relationship with him or would you just keep quiet and ignore?"

"My mom used to scream at me for telling lies."

"That is different. Parents are allowed to discipline their children and teach them the right things. Remember, you are not alone in this world, circumstances change every minute, conditions change, so it is parents' responsibility to educate their children to cope with life. Your mom was doing exactly that. I am talking about others. The main question is how would you react?"

"I don't know. It all depends on the circumstances."

"So true, one thing though you have to keep in mind is that the other person might not be intentionally telling lies," I said, "if you think for a few seconds, you might realize that there is no point in accusing someone of lying. Does it do any good? No matter what the circumstances are, just try to ignore and let it go."

"But if I know for sure that he is lying, then why should I ignore?"

"Like I said before, will it do you any good to accuse someone of lying? All it will do is create ill feelings. Just ignore it. And if you think that person is a liar, don't associate with him anymore."

"Alright, next question."

"The second question was do you take what is not yours? If someone else steals, then this particular issue basically does not affect you as long as you mind your own business," I prompted, "your obligation as a Good Samaritan always stays and if you happen to be a witness to a committed crime, then you should report. You don't necessarily have to, but it would be a good thing. So, now comes the third question. What would you do if someone hurts or harms you? Do you retaliate and go for revenge? Or do you forgive and forget?"

Meili gave me a suspicious look, "That is hard to say. I honestly don't know what I would do."

I smiled at her, it actually made me feel good that Meili was so honest, "Okay, let me remind you of our earlier conversation. You said that once when you and Mary were playing a video game, you said something that hurt Mary. Now what if Mary had said something that would have hurt you, then what would you have done? At least Mary was kind enough not to say anything, or did she?"

"No, Mary didn't say anything, but I could sense the hurt on her face," Meili replied, "as for me, I don't know what I would have done."

"That is not good enough," I said, "I'll quote you a phrase by Alexander Pope which says, 'To err is human, to forgive divine' which means people make mistakes, God forgives them, when people forgive, they are acting in a divine way. Your remark sounds like lack of confidence and a trace of vendetta. If you are trying to learn something from me, then remember that revenge will not bring you any justice. Mary's example was simple. What if somebody physically hurts you? Do you fight back or do you just defend yourself from further harm? Whatever you do, just do not go for revenge, it could kill you. There is an old Chinese saying, your mom probably knows it, I do not know verbatim, but it says something like, 'Before you go on a vendetta trip, make sure to dig two graves.'"

"How do you know that saying?" ShuYa asked. "The actual words by Confucius are 'Before you embark on a journey of revenge, dig two graves.'"

"Thank you, I'll remember that. I heard it somewhere and it got saved in my memory bank," I replied, "you see, human mind is unique, it saves everything, that is why your mind is your worst enemy. If you cannot control your mind then you could face total disaster."

"You are starting to sound like a philosopher," Meili piped in.

"No, I don't, I am only telling you what I think."

"Well, you said that very nicely, I hope Meili gets it, what is next." ShuYa again.

I relaxed a bit, trying to think of what I just said. Did I say something out of the ordinary or was it my imagination? "Well?" Meili distracted my thinking.

"Well, the next question was jealousy and greed," I said, "this one we already discussed and there is not much to add. If you could understand and follow the simple principle, then you are two steps closer to finding God."

"Okay, who is God?" Meili asked. "You haven't answered that. What is your version of God?"

Before I could answer, ShuYa got up. "We have to go, Meili, it is getting late," she said, "I promised Mary's mom to take her for shopping tomorrow."

That ended our conversation for the day but before they left, Meili said to me, "Can we talk about God next weekend?"

"Sure. You have a whole week to read on the internet all about God and more."

Afterwards, I realized that what I told them about religion might not go well with others and hoped Meili would not go around talking about religion to others. She had such a good memory that she would not forget a word of what I had said. Yet it amazed me that Meili sat there and very enthusiastically participated in our conversation. Did she really want to know about religion and God?

The next weekend never came for another six months. Summer and autumn passed by. We did lots of traveling; visiting many places in Alberta, Ontario, and Quebec. Besides taking a month off from work, almost every weekend we would go visit different places.

It was late November, four years after I first saw ShuYa, we were playing Monopoly, the weather outside was extremely severe, snowfall and freezing cold which prevented us from going out. Halfway through the game, Meili suddenly remarked, "Many months have passed and you still haven't told us about God. Can we talk about God?"

"What about the game?"

"I am tired and don't feel like playing anymore."

ShuYa got upset, "Meili, it was your idea that we play Monopoly. Now we have to finish this game."

"Mom, it will take hours to finish this game," Meili pleaded, "I don't want to play anymore."

To stop the argument, I said, "It's okay, we don't have to finish the game. We will continue some other day."

We sat there for a few minutes absolutely silent, looking at each other, then ShuYa got off the table where we were playing Monopoly and asked if we wanted some ice cream. Meili said yes and I settled for a cup of tea.

Five minutes later we were seated on the couch, Meili right next to me, staring at me with a glint in her eyes. So beautiful, almost fifteen, intelligent, smart, yet so naive. She was certainly not an outgoing type, instead she would stay home and read.

"Please tell me about God," Meili pleaded.

"There are a variety of meanings of the word God," I started, "God, as I see it, is a title given to a mega force of energy, thus has no physical or visual form. Like the sky, it is just a title or name given to an expanse of space that surrounds the earth. There is no such thing as sky, which could someday break and fall on the earth," I paused to see if Meili was paying attention.

"Go on, I am listening," she said quietly.

"Many religions conceive God as a supreme being," I continued, "people worship God as creator of the universe, perfect in everything: power, goodness, wisdom, etc. Scientists and philosophers have argued for and against the existence of God, scriptures relate many miracles performed by humans claiming them to be God's wish or command. To me, God is simple. God is everything and everything is God. God is infinite and uncountable, at the same time God is one. God is light and dark, good and evil, It knows no distinction. It comprises all, yet the origin of universe and human life is a great mystery."

"What about Darwin's theory of evolution?" Meili asked.

"So, you know about Darwin," I said, "did you learn in school the theory of evolution or did you read about it?"

Meili looked at me as if puzzled, "We came across Darwin's theory in science class, but I didn't quite get it so I read on Wikipedia. And I still don't quite get it."

"Great. That makes two of us," I smiled, but Meili just looked at me. "Okay, Darwin's theory basically says that all living beings evolved from more primitive species over time and the evolution is by natural selection. Don't ask me to explain this, you can read the explanation on internet. I just wonder, if humans evolved from some primitive species and closest to humans are monkeys, then how come humans haven't evolved yet to something else like maybe some kind of aliens, or maybe it is still too early for humans to evolve—only 200,000 years? Or maybe they are evolving so slow that we can't notice or maybe humans are the last of its kind and there is no more evolution. Is this the final frontier?"

The girls started laughing, "That's funny, so many maybes."

"Did I just crack a joke?" I asked. "Seriously, it is not funny. Just think for a minute, did humans really evolve from monkeys? Or something else? Can I actually proclaim that billions of years ago my ancestors were fish?"

More laughter followed so we decided to take a break. I went to the balcony to check the weather while ShuYa went to the kitchen to get some munchies. Meili, of course, grabbed her laptop and started reading something which I never found out.

After ten minutes, our conversation resumed. ShuYa now sat beside us and said, "I think there is a flow in your reasoning, humans are evolving. We came from Stone Age and look at us today, we are now in an electronic age. Don't you call that evolving?"

"I call that progress," I said.

"Isn't progress an evolution?"

"Sure it is," I said, "but that is material progress, to be precise. Of course, humans have come a long way from the Stone Age: we live longer, we live a healthy life, our medical science has advanced to an extent that we can cure many diseases, we have created things for our comfort and a lot more, but have we really evolved emotionally? We know that everything that changes over time is evolution."

"Our brain has."

"That is a debatable issue," Meili said, "our brain sure has. From ignorance to learned, from dumb to smart, and so on. But we are not going to argue about it. Let's leave Darwin aside and continue with God. You said God is infinite. I can understand that IF God is a powerful energy, then energy is infinite. But, how do you explain that God is everything and everything is God."

Surprised, I looked at Meili. I could not believe that she remembered word by word what I had said earlier. "Doesn't everything comprise of energy? The real question is, can you make the distinction between physical energy and the inner energy within you? If you can, then you will understand what and who God is."

"And how do you do that?"

"Find yourself," I said, "first, try to understand the difference between outer energy and inner energy, then ask yourself 'who am I?'"

"I am Meili."

"Sure you are," I said, "that is your name, your identity, but do you know who you really are?"

"Am I someone else?" Meili asked. "How do I find myself?"

"That is a gigantic question," I replied, "but let's go back a little. Do you understand the energy part?"

"I know what energy is. We all need energy to survive."

"I will try to explain what I am talking about," I said, "what you just said is correct, but that is an outer energy. With sunlight and heat, plants convert carbon dioxide and water into various energy storing compounds. When these plants are eaten, energy is transferred into animals and so on. But we are not concerned with outer energy, there is electrical energy, there is atomic energy and more, we want to find our inner energy to find God, because God is within us. If we can find ourselves, then we find our inner energy which I will call 'soul' and thus we find God."

Meili and ShuYa both looked startled, not saying anything for a few minutes. Meili finally asked, "So that is how God is everything and everything is God?"

"I think so, don't you?" I prompted, "look at it this way, you have that inner energy, we all do, which is part of the mega energy, like a glass of water which is part of a huge sea. So, you are a part of God. Find your soul and you have found God."

It was nearing midnight, I felt tired of talking and from the look on ShuYa's face, I knew that she was also tired. She finally mentioned the time and said it was time to go to bed, but Meili objected saying she had more questions from what had transpired so far.

"What has transpired so far is my opinion of God and how to find God," I said, "if you have more questions with my interpretation, we can postpone for now and we shall continue some other day. I am tired and so is your mom."

That ended our conversation but late in bed I realized that the subject of religion and God was something I had never discussed with anybody. These topics are very sensitive as everybody has their own beliefs and interpretation of God, thus every discussion turns into an argument which proves nothing and creates ill feelings. So why was I telling Meili about God? Was I out of my mind or the young, naive girl's inquisitiveness dug deep into my heart to reveal what had been buried for many years? Did it have to come out? Did I really want to talk about God? So, what happened—was it Meili or was it me? I had been extremely careful my whole life not to fall into an argument, whether about God or anything else so that I could not hurt others. I remember once Julie told me that I talk a lot yet say nothing. How ironic, now I was talking and hoping that whatever came out of my mouth did not hurt a young girl.

Lights out, I fell asleep.

Almost a month passed and there were no more questions from Meili, which was quite a relief for me. The day after our last conversation, Meili's friend Mary came by and the girls kept themselves busy in her room. Rest of the month passed by as Meili got more involved in her studies.

December was coming to an end when Meili remembered her questions. It was a quiet night, holiday season was fast approaching its end, we had just finished our dinner, Meili picked up the dishes and said, "Hey, Arif, do you remember, like, we never finished our talk about God. There are a few questions that still bother me. Can we talk about them?"

"Sure we can," I replied, "but let's clean up first."

Fifteen minutes later, we were seated in the living room when Meili asked, "You said God is within us, God is everywhere, God is infinite, and to find God, we have to find ourselves. So, first, how do we find ourselves? And if we do find ourselves, we find God, then what?" Meili paused and looked at me. When I said nothing, she continued, "Now comes the second question, if God created us then why did He do that, what does God want? After all, God is infinite, which means God is beyond time and space, so why bother creating something that is totally useless?"

I was speechless, she raised one question that had always bothered me my whole life. What does God want? I did come up with one reason, but do I want to bring it to light at this early stage of our conversation? ShuYa in the meantime laughed and said, "Meili, you think we are totally useless?"

"Aren't we?" Meili replied. "Why are we here? To grow up, get married, make kids, get old, and die? Maybe invent or create something and add our share to progress? But what good is all that?"

I sat there, didn't know what to say. Did I really want to answer that question when I myself had doubts about what God's intentions were? Meili and ShuYa were both anxiously looking at me, waiting for me to say something. Did Meili really think I was some kind of holy man that I would know all the answers about God?

"Well?" Meili prompted.

"First of all," I said, "tell me where did you find these questions? Have you been searching the internet so you can come up with questions to torment me?"

Meili looked hurt. She shifted her position on the couch to look at me. "I am sorry," she said, "I didn't mean to torment you. I had been searching the internet for a long time, read about many different religions and different versions of God, and guess what? I am more confused than ever before. I liked the way you explained God, I believe in you and I think you are wonderful. You say things that actually make sense. I came up with these questions because

I want to learn, and I have faith in you and I know deep in my heart that you will answer them honestly and truthfully."

Those words uttered by a fifteen-year-old girl touched my heart. I almost had tears in my eyes. I finally said, "Thank you, my dear, I will try my best."

ShuYa, sensing uneasiness, got up and went to the kitchen, saying she was going to make some tea. Meili went and got some ice cream for herself. The break gave me some time to compose myself and decide how I would explain the intricate subject of God.

"We will start with your first question," I said to Meili after we had our break, "how to find yourself to find God and when you find God you can ask Him what He wants." I smiled. That, of course, didn't go well with Meili. I could tell from the look she gave me. "Okay, don't give me that dirty look, can't I joke?" I continued, "Remember the first two steps we talked about, what was it, six or so months ago?"

"I remember," Meili promptly replied, "the one about truth, stealing, and jealousy."

"Right. Are you following them?"

"I am trying but sometimes I deviate. I think it is into humans not to be perfect."

"Those steps are not meant to make you perfect," I said, "they make you a good person. After you master the art of being a good person, comes step number three."

"Which is?" Meili asked.

"Your ego."

Meili right away opened her laptop to check the meaning of ego, which was good because it meant she was

41

anxious to learn, but surprised me that she did not know what ego meant.

"It says here ego means, 'A person's sense of self-esteem or self-importance' and lots more."

"Great, we got the meaning of ego," I said, "but do you understand what that means?"

"You explain."

"Ego is your opinion of yourself. Are you better than others, do you think you are important and have great abilities?" I tried to explain, "Ego, basically, is sense of your own worth, which is the main cause of hate and fear."

"Okay, so what about ego?"

"You have to let it go, get it out of your mind completely," I said, "because you are nothing, it is only your own sense of importance, which is a delusion. Did you not say we are useless? In reality, it all boils down to our physical existence and has nothing to do with our soul except our body which houses it, therefore we need to take care of our body. Clear your mind of worldly affairs, don't worry about things you have to do or things that are happening around you or elsewhere."

During the entire conversation between Meili and I, ShuYa had been patiently listening, not saying anything. Finally, she said, "That is easier said than done. We do have to live our life and all the obstacles we encounter doing that have to be overcome. Our mind is always clogged up with worldly affairs."

"Very true," I said, "but worldly affairs are irrelevant, it is your sense of self that matters and that is what you have to let go. Once you do that, you will understand that nothing really matters. You will realize that the world is just an illusion like your dreams because what you see in your dreams disappears when you wake up. You have to wake up from worldly dreams and look within you to see the soul because your soul has lived through all that. For your soul, time does not exist. There is no past, present, or future—"

Meili at this point interrupted by saying, "So, is that how we find God?"

"Exactly."

"Okay, can we talk about soul," Meili asked, "what is all this about time and past and present."

"Subject of soul is very complex," I said, "it will take time to explain and right now, we don't have time to go into it. Some day we will talk about soul. For now, just concentrate on those three steps we discussed, try to understand them and follow them. Become a good person first, then we go into soul and the ways to find your soul. You cannot go to university before completing your high school."

That was the end of our conversation for the night.

What was I doing, I thought to myself later on, opening a can of worms? I was sure Meili would come up with hundreds of questions.

Chapter 5

Meili turned sixteen. For many months, we did not discuss or talk about God or soul. For the last fifteen months, she kept to herself, did not talk much. She concentrated on her studies. Even during last summer break she read a lot, hardly played her favorite video games, hardly went out, or visit Mary. I could sense a big change in her behavior from the way she acted, the way she talked. Her attitude changed drastically. Before, she always was a helping hand to her mother, but now she went out of her way to please her mother and me. Sometimes, she would ask me three, four times if I would like a cup of coffee or tea. She even cleaned up her room, which normally looked like it had been hit by a hurricane. ShuYa, towards the end of summer, told me that I brainwashed her, which was kind of funny because Meili always was a good girl, obedient and caring. I told ShuYa that she was evolving as she was maturing, but ShuYa just laughed and said we were not going to talk about evolution.

Spring finally arrived. ShuYa and I were planting flowers on the balcony when Meili joined us and very quietly asked me if I was available to talk about soul.

"How come it took you almost a year and a half to bring up the subject of soul?" I asked.

"I wasn't ready for it."

"Okay, we'll talk about it after supper."

The hot mid-April day started to turn cooler after the sunset, so we packed up and went indoors. Meili had already set up the dinner table.

"Meili, you said you weren't ready before," I said after we settled down, "are you ready now?"

"I think so."

"Okay, tell me what you found out about soul in all these months," I asked, "how much did you read and what is the outcome?"

"I read a little bit," Meili said, "but you said I have to first work on those three steps we discussed."

"I am glad to hear that, and how is it going?"

"I am still working on it."

"See what I told you," ShuYa said with a smile on her face, "Meili has changed."

"No, I haven't."

"Changing to become a good person is one of the most difficult things to do," I said, "you need courage, will, and incentive to do that. Your thought process and your activities have to be adjusted, at the same time you have to make sure that you don't get cheated by others because you still have to live your life."

"You mean be a good person," Meili said, "but don't become a monk?"

"Not quite the same," I said, "monks live alone by themselves in the monastery, but they have a purpose. We have a purpose too, yet we live in an outside world and spiritual life is not the only way to live. We still have a physical life to live."

"Okay, we have to live both lives," Meili said, turning towards me, "physical I understand, how do we manage the spiritual? Is this where soul comes in?"

"Yes, but you still haven't told me what you found out about soul?" I asked.

Meili just sat there, not saying anything. I thought she was probably trying to figure out how to phrase words when suddenly she jumped up from the couch and ran to her room. A few minutes later, she came back with a whole bunch of papers in her hands. She sat down, flipped through the pages, reading while ShuYa and I patiently waited for her to say something.

"Soul is also called spirit," Meili said, "I guess that's why you said spiritual life. Soul is the part of you that makes you who you are and is located in your heart or lungs or brain. Where exactly, I have no idea and can't be found in your anatomy either. All body parts are known and located within the human body and animals as well, yet the location of the soul is a mystery."

"That is a good start," I said, "I see you referred to your notes. Can I see them?"

"Of course you can."

She handed me all her papers and laughed. I did not have a clue why she laughed until I saw her notes; they were written in Chinese and she knew I can't read Chinese. Yes, she pulled a fast one on me, so I said politely, "Thank you, that is very nice of you, so now you'll have to read them to me."

ShuYa was looking at me, full of curiosity, I figured. "The notes are in Chinese," I told her. She started laughing too. For nothing better to do, I joined them, and suddenly we were all happily laughing.

"Okay, read some more," I said to Meili after we had had a good laugh.

"The soul is immortal," Meili read from her notes, "thus the soul lives after death. That's it, your turn now."

"You did good," I told Meili, "let's start with the soul being a spirit, thus it is invisible which is why it cannot be found within the anatomy of your body—but you can find it. The location of the soul in your body is not important because your inner energy is everywhere within your body. Do not confuse soul with heart or your mind. Your heart is associated with your emotions while the mind is with your thinking and reasoning, but the soul is strictly spiritual and has very little to do with your physical life. You live your life and depending on how you live that life affects your spiritual life."

"How so?"

"Okay, let's go back to those three steps," I tried to explain, "if you live your life strictly by those rules, then you have achieved what I call 'awakening,' which is absolutely necessary for your spiritual life. Your thinking process and your actions are in control and you are looking at the world from a different perspective."

Meili wrote some more in her notes while ShuYa politely got up and gestured me to join her in the kitchen. "Do you think you can explain to her what different perspective you are talking about?" she whispered.

"I'll try if she asks," I whispered back.

47

Meili was waiting for us to return and before I could sit down, she said, "What was all the whispering about? I am not deaf, you know, I could hear you guys in the kitchen."

"It was nothing, we were whispering because we did not want to disturb you," ShuYa said as I sat down.

"Fine," Meili said with disbelief, "I don't understand the part where you said we look at the world from a different perspective, can you explain?"

"Sure," I looked at ShuYa, she was smiling, "a normal person likes or dislikes something, hates or loves something and so on, but when you achieve awakening, you will feel the love within you, birds chirping will be music to your ears, you'll love plants and animals, you'll appreciate the beauty and scent of flowers, you'll feel sorry for the homeless people, you'll feel compassion for the crippled and sick, and your overall view on life will be more inclined towards the wellbeing of others. These are only few things for example, but there would be many different aspects of life that you will be looking at differently."

Meili gave me a puzzled look, "Okay, so does this mean you become a spiritual person?" she finally asked.

"Something like that."

"What about the soul then?" she asked, "where did we lose it and how does it come into the picture?"

"We haven't lost it yet, but then, we haven't found it either, we are working on it," I said, turning towards the balcony, "why don't we go out and have some fresh air, we can check out the moon and stars."

ShuYa looked out the window and said, "There are no stars or moon, only a dark sky with lots of clouds."

"Arif is stalling," Meili said, "do we have a problem with the soul?"

"No, we don't have a problem but if you think I am stalling then you have no idea how long it will take to find your soul."

"How long?"

"Probably years."

"No way!" Meili exclaimed. "Is it really that hard?"

"Yes," I said, "let me tell you about the soul first, then we'll talk about finding it. Your spiritual life is strictly your inner self, which means your inner feelings overrule your conscious reasoning. Some people call it intuition, I call it advice from your soul."

Meili looked puzzled and so did ShuYa, while I sat there smiling, which was a bad idea because Meili irritably said, "You are joking. How can your instinct be advice from your soul?"

"How often do you get an instinct to do or say something?"

"Not very often."

"You know why? Because your soul doesn't talk to you all the time, only in extraneous circumstances. Your soul is trying to help you since your soul represents the meaning and purpose of your existence."

"There you go, Meili," ShuYa said laughing, "do you still think we are useless?"

"Yes," Meili turned towards her mother, "the way Arif is explaining, we are useless until we find our soul or God and the way I understand is THAT is the meaning and purpose of our existence. Our life should be devoted to finding God."

"You got that almost right. High-five!" I said, raising my hand.

"Alright," Meili jumped off the couch and clapped my hand.

Disgusted, ShuYa said, "You guys are nuts."

"No, we are just happy," I said, "but don't forget, you still have to live your physical life and live that life in peace and harmony and be happy."

Thus ended our conversation for the night. ShuYa got up and walked to the balcony saying that was enough for the day. I checked the time, it was after eleven. Strange how time goes by so fast when we have a serious talk. Meili, of course, was not done yet but respected her mother's decision. We got up and joined ShuYa on the balcony. The night was cool, clouds had moved away leaving the sky clear. We sat there for several minutes, nobody said a word, and then finally we packed up for the night.

One Friday evening in late June, over two months after we had had our last conversation, Meili asked me if we could go for a walk in the park. ShuYa opted out which was understandable as she walked to work downtown every day and back. Meili and I walked to the nearby park; grass was green, people walking, kids riding bicycles, dogs in their confined areas running loose, young boys and girls playing baseball, some people sitting on benches in the shade and overall it was a beautiful walk. It was also nice to see that people were enjoying a warm day in the park.

"Let's go sit over there," Meili said, pointing towards a huge tree after we had walked for about twenty minutes.

"Where do we sit, there is no bench there?"

"We sit on the grass under that tree."

"That is a good idea, let's do that."

We made ourselves comfortable under the huge poplar tree. I stretched my legs and leaned back against the stem of the tree, Meili did the same beside me. We sat there for a while not saying a word, just observing the beauty of the green park. Sky had turned orange and yellow on the horizon where the sun was getting ready to disappear.

"Arif, are you happy with your life?" Meili suddenly asked.

"I have no complaints," I said, turning towards her, "God has given me everything I need and then some. Why do you ask?"

"Because some time back you said live in peace and be happy, so how many people do you know that are happy?"

"Happiness is just a frame of mind. If you think you are happy then you are happy, but if you think you don't have enough and want more, you are greedy, then you will never be happy," I said, trying to explain as best as I could. "Happiness can be defined in many ways. Sometimes you are happy doing things you like or maybe you are with a person, you enjoy his company and you feel happy. Basically, happiness is a state of well-being and contentment. I know one person who I think is happy."

"Who?"

"Your mom, and the rest of the people don't matter."

"You think my mom is happy?"

"Don't you think so?" I said. "Have you ever noticed, she never complains about anything, never asks for anything, and is always there when you need her. I think she is content with her life."

"That means she is a good person, but is she happy?" Meili asked. "How can you tell?"

"I can't, but I think she is happy with her life," I replied, "and we should not be talking about her in her absence."

"Why can't I talk about her, she is my mom?"

"Indeed, she is," I said facing her, "but to talk about other people in their absence is not right. I am sorry I mentioned your mom."

"No, no, don't be," Meili said soothingly, "I know my mom is the best. I feel so lucky to have her as my mother."

The sun had set, people were leaving the park, so I said to Meili, "We should go now, it's getting dark."

"Sure," Meili got up.

ShuYa was working on her computer when we got back. Meili ran over to her and kissed her. Surprised, ShuYa looked at me and said, "What happened, did I miss something?"

"No, Mom, I love you."

"Okay, what's up? Why the sudden affection, what did I do?"

"Nothing."

I thought that was enough, so I said to ShuYa, "You know there is a saying, 'Curiosity killed the cat.' Do not push it, we had a wonderful walk, and nothing really happened."

"Yeah, Mom, nothing happened, we missed you."

ShuYa finally smiled and said, "Thank you."

Weekend went by, so did the next two weeks before Meili came back with her questions. We were watching a movie on TV, ShuYa was half-asleep on the sofa while Meili was reading a book about cats, when suddenly she decided she had had enough of cats and came to sit near me. She whispered in my ear, "Can we talk about soul?"

"Do you want to?" I whispered back.

"I would love to."

So much for whispering, ShuYa got up and said, "Wait, I want to be a part of that conversation. Let me get some tea first."

"What I am going to explain and everything I have said so far for the last couple of years is my own version of soul," I said after ShuYa brought us tea, "it is not meant as philosophical or scientific. You can find thousands of books by great philosophers and scientists that have put forward theories and explanations of soul, God, and enlightenment. I am nowhere close to them, I am just an ordinary person who believes in truth, honesty, and righteousness." I paused to sip some tea. "What I have told you is not going to hurt you," I continued, "and if you can learn from it that would be nice or you can completely ignore it. Whatever you decide, just don't go crazy about it."

"I want to learn," Meili immediately responded, "I want to find God, not from all the books but from you."

"You please my heart, you are so kind. God, you will have to find by yourself, I can only show you the way," I said. It was hard to imagine that little girl had so much faith in me. She was quite mature and intelligent, she read lots of books of wisdom, philosophy, and science, yet she had come to me to learn about God. I only wished I could live up to her expectations and hoped I could explain to her my views in simple terms so that I would not disappoint her.

ShuYa again must have sensed my uneasiness because she said, "You don't have to be too precise, just express your views. I am sure Meili will understand."

"Okay, let's review from the beginning," I started, "we talked about soul being a spirit, infinite, and part of God. Barring Darwin's theory, why God created living beings and what does God want is still a mystery. I wish I could answer that question. Only reason I can think of is that God wants all of us to know Him, that's why God put part of Himself into us, this is the purpose of our life—find ourselves, and we find God."

Did I know what I was talking about or did I realize that I had just said what I really never wanted to discuss? ShuYa and Meili were patiently listening, not saying anything.

"I know it sounds ridiculous," I continued after I finished my tea, "but think for a minute, what other reason could there be?"

"If that is the reason why God created us," Meili said, "then I don't understand why would He do that? Is He looking for glory for His artwork? And from His own creation yet?"

"You sure raise interesting questions," I said, "to be honest, I don't have an answer to that, maybe someday we'll find out. For now, I could think of one possibility why God wants to evolve."

"Are we going back to evolution?" ShuYa asked.

"That sounds funny," Meili said, laughing. "God is infinite, so why would God want to evolve?"

"Infinite doesn't necessarily mean unable to evolve, does it?" I said. "After all, infinity+1 still equals infinity. As for evolution," I faced ShuYa, "we know that every living being evolves, when I said a long time ago that my ancestors were fish, I was only kidding, but it could be a possibility. Look out on the balcony, the seeds we planted three months ago became plants and now we have flowers, some plants become huge trees, look at humans, they all grow up, we already discussed that is evolution. The definition of evolution, if you check the dictionary, you'll find many versions, but basically it means 'A process of continuous change.'"

"So, you are suggesting that God wants to change, become bigger, or something else?" Meili again.

"Maybe," I said, "it is a theory."

"Okay, let's leave God out for now and go back to soul," Meili said, "tell us more about soul and how to find it."

"I am so sorry, my mind is all cluttered up right now," I said, "can we talk about soul tomorrow?"

"We will not make it tomorrow," ShuYa said.

"Why not?" I asked.

"We are going to the mall for shopping, Meili needs some new clothes, you know, she is going to high school this coming September."

"Shopping is during the day time, we can talk at night," I said.

"I thought we were going out for dinner tomorrow night," ShuYa responded.

"Okay then, we'll talk some other time," I said, "I really don't feel like talking right now."

Meili put her hand on my shoulder and said soothingly, "It's fine, no problem, we will talk some other time. And by the way, will you come with us for shopping?"

"I'll come to the mall but I am not going shopping," I said, "I don't like shopping, I'll wait at the food court."

Bright and early next morning, Saturday, we left at eleven o'clock for the mall. It was early for me because I always sleep-in on the weekends while girls go for grocery shopping. I was totally barred from going grocery shopping except when ShuYa needed help carrying twenty kg bag of rice and at that I was not allowed to touch anything in the store. Few years back, one day when Meili was still small, we went for grocery shopping. I was designated to push the shopping cart with Meili while ShuYa picked the fruits and veggies and meat. By the time we reached the cashier, our shopping cart was full, not with veggies and fruits but mostly junk food. Meili and I got everything from potato chips—many flavors—nachos and tortillas, peanuts, cashews, dry Indian and Chinese snacks, chocolate bars to ice-cream, pastries to cookies. You name it, we had it in our shopping cart. Meili was quite happy but ShuYa was not. She, of course, did not say anything at the store but when we got home, she told me "you will not be going grocery shopping anymore." I thought she was kidding, so a week later I got ready for the shopping trip but ShuYa reminded me what she had told me earlier. I protested but all she said was it was for our own good.

"Look at Meili," she said, "a whole week she has eaten nothing but junk food. By the time she is twenty, she will be fat and diabetic."

No further discussion, I went back to bed and since then I was prohibited from going grocery shopping. Once in a while, ShuYa would bring some munchies just to keep us happy.

We got to the mall forty minutes later, parked the vehicle one kilometer away, the parking lot was full, and walked in. Girls went shopping while I headed to the food court. The place was so crowded that it took me ten minutes to find a table to sit down. So much for recession! I must have walked around the food kiosks at least three times before I could decide what I was going to eat. Burgers looked very tempting, so did everything else but then it occurred to me that if ShuYa saw me eating more junk food, she would probably give me a dirty look, so I got rice, veggies, and chicken from Edo. While I was eating, a thought came to my mind, why does everybody have to eat at noon? Why don't we just eat when we are hungry instead of twelve o'clock? Are we really slaves to our clock? Does the time override our stomach? Even at work, twelve o'clock, everybody stops working, lunchtime! I once asked my partner why he always has to stop for lunch at noon, why can't he eat his lunch when he gets hungry and he said he gets hungry at twelve. So, if I turned the clock two hours ahead, I wonder if he would still be hungry at twelve. Suddenly, my plate was empty, I must have gobbled down my food while I was thinking about time. Yes, time, time, time, we even change the clock back and forth every six months or so, yet people still eat lunch at noon, that one hour we changed on our clock just does not count. Sure, we change the clock at midnight and either gain an extra hour's sleep or lose an hour, but how does our stomach know that twelve o'clock is lunchtime? It must be psychological, we have trained our mind to send a message to our stomach that noon is the time to get hungry.

My thinking got interrupted when I felt a tug on my ear lobe, I turned around to find ShuYa and Meili standing behind me.

"What did you eat?" ShuYa asked. "We are hungry too."

"Done shopping?" I asked. "That was quick."

"Not yet, we want to eat first."

"What would you like?"

"What did you have?"

"Chicken with rice and veggies."

"I want that," Meili said, "where did you get it from?"

"There," I said, pointing a finger at Edo. "Sit down, I'll get you some. How about you?" I asked ShuYa.

"Sure."

Half an hour later, the girls went back shopping while I moved to the central court, found myself a bench, and sat down. Enough with the food court. People all around me walking, shopping, and doing whatever they felt like. With our economy on the verge of disaster, it sure felt strange that so many people still spent money shopping. I guessed kids were growing up fast and needed new clothes for school like Meili. Yes, that little three-foot girl just five years ago is now over five feet tall and even more beautiful than her mother. Meili sure has all the characteristics of her mother. Particularly in the last two years, she has become more polite and gentle. Has she really changed as her mother claimed or was she always like that but never showed any signs? She was always reserved and self-centered, hardly talked with anybody, yet was always helpful to her mother.

I was sitting there on the bench thinking about Meili when a sweet little old lady came and sat beside me. About five feet tall, very slim, with short gray hair, long wrinkly face and hands, must be over ninety years old yet her voice was like a twenty-year girl, "Are you waiting for somebody?" she asked me politely.

"Yes, Ma'am," I replied, "I am waiting for my family. They are gone shopping."

"So nice of you," she said, "I don't have any family, my husband passed away three years ago and left me all alone."

"I am so sorry," I said, "didn't you have any children?"

"No, God wasn't gracious to us."

It sounded so strange that we blamed God for our misfortunes and praised the Lord in opposite circumstances. Was God the culprit or was it our own doing? Did our soul have anything to do with our mishaps? "I am sure your husband's spirit is always with you," I said, trying to comfort the little lady. "How did he die, was it old age or something else?"

"You are so kind," she had tears in her eyes. "Yes, my husband is always with me, he even talks to me some nights when I feel lonely. He had appendicitis and the doctors could not diagnose in time, it burst and killed him. Can I buy you coffee?"

"Thank you so much," I said, "I'll get the coffee. What do you take in your coffee?"

"Little milk, please."

I got up and went to get coffee. I remembered seeing Tim Hortons at the food court, so headed over there. Few minutes later, I was back with two coffees, but the old lady was gone. Surprised, I looked around, the little lady was nowhere in sight. But I did find a piece of paper on the bench with scribbled letters, 'thank you for the coffee.' I sat down wondering who she was, where did she come from, and where did she disappear? Why me? Why would she relate her sad story to me? Was she trying to tell me something? But what? Or maybe she was just a stranger passing by, taking a break to relax for a few minutes.

The girls came back and the first question ShuYa asked me was how come I was drinking coffee from two cups at the same time. "One wasn't enough," I said.

"Good answer," Meili laughed.

"Done shopping?" I asked. "What did you get?"

"Couple of jeans, shirts, and a pair of shoes."

"Good, can we go now?"

Four days later, Meili had gone to visit Mary, ShuYa was catching up on her accounting updates on the computer, so I made a bowl of popcorn, left half for ShuYa, and went to the balcony. It was a hot summer day, the sun was still shining. I sat down to watch people walking, jogging, and walking dogs when suddenly I saw a little old lady. She looked up—we were on the third floor—and waved at me. I waved back, smiling, and then it dawned on me. I had seen that old lady before. She was the same one from the mall few days ago. I got up and shouted, "Wait for me," and ran out, three flights of stairs and I was out on the street. The old woman was nowhere in sight. I ran to the next block but couldn't find her. Disappointed, I walked back slowly.

ShuYa was waiting for me at the door when I got back. "What was all that about?" she asked. "Who was that?"

"Come out with me on the balcony and I'll tell you."

We sat down, and I told her about the incident at the mall and why I had two cups of coffee. "Just now, a few minutes ago, I saw her downstairs on the sidewalk and she waved at me," I said.

"Is that why you ran down?"

"Yeah, but she was gone, I couldn't find her."

"Maybe you just imagined it," ShuYa pointed out.

"Could be, but do you think the mall incident was also my imagination?"

"Why not?"

I dug into my wallet and brought out the piece of paper I had found on the bench at the mall. "How would you explain this?" I asked ShuYa, handing her the paper.

"Okay, the mall incident was not your imagination," ShuYa said after she read the note. "Just forget about it and, by the way, why are you keeping this note?"

"I don't know, I just put it in my wallet the other day," I said, "but it sure feels strange, that old woman showed up again and then disappeared."

Weekend came, and we continued our conversation. ShuYa decided we had had enough adventure the previous Saturday so we would stay home this time and have a peaceful evening doing nothing.

Meili started the conversation, "Are we now going to continue with soul?"

"Sure," I said, "what do you remember about soul that we discussed?"

"Everything so far."

"Okay, now we get to the last chapter about soul." I looked at ShuYa, she was smiling. An encouraging smile, I thought. "Our soul," I continued, "has lived many lives; past, present, and future, therefore time does not exist. It is one straight line and our present physical life could be anywhere on that line, we don't know exactly where."

"Woah, woah, slow down," Meili interrupted. "I have a couple of questions regarding what you just said. First, if soul has lived all those lives, then why is it doing it again and second, we live our life the way we like, we make all sorts of decisions every day and maybe if we make a different decision other than what we should have made, our life moves in a different direction, so how does soul know that and how could it have lived that particular life?"

"Interesting," ShuYa prompted, "that is a very good question."

"It is, and I am glad you are following me," I said. "Your first question; by living all those lives, soul is gaining knowledge and experience, which it needs to evolve into a higher soul and the second question; everyday of our life, we come across different issues and decisions we have to make. Most of the time, there are a whole bunch of options that we can choose from, I call them different paths, and no matter which path we choose, our soul has lived through it all."

"I'm like, having difficulty understanding that, but maybe someday you'll explain it more clearly," Meili said, "for now, tell me what a higher soul is?"

"Higher soul is what we call an angel," I answered, "its purpose is to help, advise, and guide the other souls."

"If our soul already has an angel, why are we wasting our time and energy to find it?"

"Because we want to find ourselves, find God, and free our soul from worldly affairs."

For a few minutes, there was total silence, both the girls were looking at me puzzled. ShuYa finally got up and declared teatime. The girls didn't drink coffee at night, so we drank green tea.

"What I just said about soul is not only extremely difficult to explain but it is also very hard to understand," I continued after our tea break. "Science might not agree with it and the philosophers would argue the concept, but it is my theory and it requires not science but a simple belief. You can choose to believe it or you can forget about it. Either way, no harm will come to you but at least by believing me you will become a better person, you will learn how to control your mind, your thinking process will alter, which will affect your activities and your life."

Meili seemed perplexed, looked at me sadly, and said, "You don't have to get so defensive, I believed you that's why I want to learn from you. So, teach me how to find my soul."

"There are many different methods to find your soul," I said, "the one I know is the easiest. It is called meditation."

"I knew it!" Meili exclaimed, "I have heard about it. So, tell me what meditation is and how do we meditate?"

"I also want to learn how to meditate," ShuYa moved closer.

"The subject of meditation will require some time," I tried to explain, "we will go into that some other time, but for now, check the dictionary and encyclopedia for the meaning of meditation."

The girls did not argue that, thus ended our talk about soul. It was hot indoors and ShuYa's suggestion of going for a short walk was welcomed. While we were walking, a cool breeze in our face, ShuYa said to me, "If you are going to teach us meditation, you'll have to do it fast. We are on holiday next month and then in September Meili goes back to school." It was mid-July so I thought we still had two weeks to finish our topic of God.

Few days later, Wednesday night I came home from my weekly bridge game at the club extremely tired. Girls were busy with their stuff, ShuYa studying and Meili reading. I excused myself and went to bed. That night I dreamed that I was back in the mall and the same little old lady came and sat beside me. This time I was sitting at the food court, having a coffee when I heard that young voice say hello. I looked at her surprised, said hello, and asked her if she would like some coffee.

"Yes, please, little milk?"

I got up and walked to the coffee shop, keeping my eyes on her to make sure that she did not disappear again. I came back with coffee but before I could give it to her, she said, "Thank you, I have to go to the washroom, could you please set it on the table?" She got up and slowly headed towards the washroom. I was tempted to follow her but unfortunately, I couldn't go to the ladies' washroom. I sat there waiting for twenty minutes, I timed it, but the old woman never came back. Couple of ladies came out of the washroom, so I asked them if a short, skinny, gray-haired old woman was in there, and they said there was nobody there. She did it again, she disappeared. I woke with a start, ShuYa was sitting beside me, pushing my shoulder.

"Wake up, wake up," ShuYa whispered.

"What?" I asked, startled. "What happened?"

"I think Meili is crying," she whispered.

Then I heard a faint sobbing sound, "Go check on her," I whispered back.

"Her door is closed."

"Why do you think she is crying? Did something happen?"

"No, nothing happened except she has been complaining of stomach ache for the last couple of days."

"Where in the stomach is the pain located?" I asked.

"She said on the right side below hip level. She also threw up a couple of times today."

"Why didn't you tell me sooner?" I asked.

"You weren't home and when you came back, you said you were tired and went to bed."

I quickly got up because it hit me then why the old lady showed up in my dreams, she came to tell me something, "Go to Meili and tell her to dress up quickly and then you get ready, we are going to the hospital," I told ShuYa and ran to call the ambulance.

Ten minutes later, the ambulance arrived and Meili was rushed to emergency. ShuYa and I followed the ambulance to the hospital in our car. When we got to the emergency after parking our car, Meili was already admitted. Usually there is a 3-4 hours wait time, but the attending nurse immediately recognized Meili's symptoms and took her inside right away and called the doctor. After the doctor had seen Meili, we were allowed to go visit her. Meili was lying on bed very pale and said nothing.

"What's wrong with my baby?" ShuYa asked me.

"We'll ask the nurse," I said, "but I think I know what it is. Don't worry, it is not serious."

"Then why the big rush?" she asked. "What is it?"

"I think it is appendicitis and a little caution won't hurt."

The lab nurse came and took blood, other nurses came and gave Meili some pills. When I asked what was wrong with Meili, she just said the doctor will explain. About forty-five minutes later, after a few more tests, the doctor showed up and explained that Meili had an acute appendicitis which was quite swollen and needed to be removed immediately, and that he had asked for the operating room to get set up. When I asked him how serious it was, he said it would be extremely serious if the appendix ruptured and it could happen any time. Two hours later, after we signed a whole bunch of papers, Meili was taken to surgery. ShuYa and I went out to the waiting room. It was already dawn and the sun was starting to rise. ShuYa was tightly holding my hand, tears running down her cheeks, and kept asking me if Meili would be alright.

An hour later, we were informed that the surgery went well and that Meili was in the recovery room. We could visit her later during the day. Relieved, ShuYa hugged me and whispered in my ear, "Thank you for saving my girl."

Three days later, Meili came home from the hospital looking fresh and healthy. While she was in the hospital, we visited her every day, ShuYa would make soup for her and bring fruits. The nursing staff at the hospital was extremely courteous and very friendly. They certainly took good care of Meili.

Chapter 6

As much as I wanted to finish our conversation within two weeks, things did not work out with Meili's surgery. We left for holiday early August for three weeks and by the time we got back, Meili, although she was feeling much better, decided it was time to prepare for her high school. I thought it was a good excuse because I had a nasty feeling that she was just getting over the shock of her surgery. She could not believe that she had been on the deathbed when ShuYa told her how serious her condition was, few days after she came home from the hospital.

Our conversation resumed in October. It was early one Saturday afternoon, girls had gone grocery shopping when I got a call from Lou asking if we would like to join him and his girlfriend Rina for dinner at an Indian restaurant. It was tempting but I remembered ShuYa had invited Mary and her mom for supper, so I asked Lou to come over and have spicy Indian food at our place. We, of course, ordered food which saved us from the trouble to cook.

After we had a hearty meal, we were sitting in the living room having ice-cream cake from DQ for dessert when Meili asked Rina, who was a religious woman, "Hey, Rina, can I ask you a simple question?"

"Sure, my dear, what would you like?"

"Do you believe in religion?"

ShuYa gave me a suspicious look, probably wondering what was going on. I had no idea what Meili was up to.

"Yes, I am a Christian," Rina replied.

"Do you go to church?"

"Yes, on Sundays."

"Tomorrow is Sunday. If you go to church, can I go with you?" Meili asked very gently.

"Certainly," Rina replied, "I'll be happy to take you with me."

"Meili, you don't need Rina to take you to church, you can go by yourself," ShuYa said.

"Of course, you can go by yourself," Rina added, "church is God's house and doors are open to all His children. I'll be glad to take you with me tomorrow."

Next morning, Rina came and took Meili to church. Later on, when ShuYa asked Meili how her experience at church was, Meili responded that she actually felt very good, peaceful, and relaxed. That night, Meili looked happy and asked me to continue with our talk about meditation.

"The subject of meditation will take much longer than just a few minutes," I said. "You have to go to school and we have to go to work tomorrow, so meditation can wait for now." I looked at ShuYa who nodded. "Your mom and I were wondering, what prompted you to go to church this morning," I continued, "and what did you learn?"

Meili looked at her mom, surprised, and said, "Ah ha, you guys were wondering? Why can't I go to church? I'm like, allowed to do that, am I not?"

"Of course you are, but why the sudden decision?"

"Well, we talked about religion way back when?" Meili replied. "I know that you believe in Islam, although you never talk about it, maybe someday you will tell me about Islam, I hope, so I decided I'll go learn about Christianity and since Rina was here I thought it was a good time to do it."

"That is great," I said, pleased that she wanted to learn. "So, what did you learn?"

"Not much," Meili replied, "but the atmosphere was so peaceful, I felt very relaxed. Only thing that I could not understand was why do Christians pray to Jesus Christ who they claim is the son of God, instead of God Himself?"

"Good question, did you not ask Rina about that? She would probably have explained it better than I could."

"I wanted to but then I remembered what we had discussed."

"And what was that?" I asked, "I don't remember discussing Christianity."

"Not Christianity," Meili replied, "the one about what others do is their business, not mine."

"Oh, that," I said, impressed that she remembered, "well, if you wanted to learn then you could have asked Rina in a polite way, like, how come she is praying to Jesus and not God instead of why is she praying to Christ. You see, that WHY makes a big difference when you phrase a question. Anyway, I'll tell you what I know but you will be able to find a lot more on the internet. Christians believe, as far as I know in 'Father, Son, and Holy Spirit' which is described as 'Trinity'—one God in three divine persons— where Father is God, Son is Jesus Christ, and Holy Spirit is the third person. So basically, when they pray to Jesus Christ, they are praying to God."

"What is Holy Spirit?" Meili asked.

"Holy Spirit is divine inspiration, the giver of life, the spirit of Christ, the spirit of truth, and so on," I said. "When you have time, read about Christianity and you'll learn more."

ShuYa at this point stretched and got up saying, "Okay, that is enough for tonight, next session will be on Saturday."

Why does it always have to be on Saturday night? It seemed to me that Saturday night was when Meili got a chance to poke into my brain. Sometimes, I wonder if my teaching is good enough or correct to help her become a better person. I could see that she certainly had changed; her attitude, her behavior, the way she talked, but she still had an inquisitive mind. Could I really help her on the journey to enlightenment?

After supper on Saturday night, we gathered in the living room, Meili sat beside me on the couch and enthusiastically asked, "Do we finally get to discuss the issue of meditation?"

"Okay, let's start from the beginning," I said. "Meditation is probably the oldest technique spiritually to attain enlightenment, to find your inner self, to find God. Meditation may also reduce stress, pain, and anxiety. It may increase self-control and self-knowledge. It will certainly help you remember those three steps we discussed a long time ago. You will find that almost every religion preaches some form of meditation." I paused to see if Meili was paying attention, "So, the big question is, what is meditation?"

ShuYa moved closer, sat facing me, and waited for me to continue. Meili also was anxiously looking at me.

"Let me start with a simple question, can your eyes see themselves?"

"Yes, if I look into the mirror."

"Exactly, your eyes need a median to see themselves. Meditation is the median to see your soul," I said. "Different traditions define meditation differently and practice differently. My definition of meditation is focusing your mind on a particular object, image, thought, activity, or even breathing; the dictionary definition, if you look it up, will say 'To focus one's mind or the act of giving your attention to only one thing' which just about says it all. Mind you, there might be many more definitions, but our discussion and my version of meditation stops right here."

"And how do you do that?" Meili asked.

"Very simple," I said, "for example, I have seen you sitting on that table trying to solve your math problems for hours and not paying any attention to anything else, which tells me that you are focused on one thing—math. Meditation is much simpler than trying to solve the math problem. The idea behind meditation is to learn to concentrate on a particular thing, to train your mind to forget the material issues and focus on that particular thing. Once your mind is trained to that level, you will lose your sense of self-esteem or your ego. You will achieve a calm state—mentally and emotionally, you will feel more relaxed which will lead you to your inner conscious. Only then you will be able to find yourself. You have learned those three steps we discussed, which are the keys to the front door, but your ego, your sense of 'I,' is the most difficult of them to let go. The first two steps are easy to learn if you decide to follow that path, but ego? That is the tough one, thus comes meditation."

"So, to concentrate on math is not enough? Wouldn't you call that meditation?" Meili asked.

"Solving a math problem requires you to use your brain to calculate, you would even refer to text-books to help solve the problem," I tried to explain, although I had no idea how clearly I could explain, "it sure gets you to focus your mind on the math problem, but meditation is not a problem that you would ponder for hours to solve it. You don't have to use your brain, you just have to relax and let everything go."

"How can you let everything go?"

"Attention control which requires practice, consistency, and desire."

"You mean we should first have the desire to let things go and then consistently practice?"

"Exactly," I said, pleased to see that Meili was into it, "that is where meditation comes into picture, it is a tool to practice to start a long journey."

"How long a journey?"

"That is entirely up to you," I said, "how soon can you open your eyes and see within you?"

"Aren't my eyes open now?"

"Yes, to material things, but are they open to see what is inside you?" I asked.

"I don't know," Meili promptly replied, "how do I see inside, wherever that is?"

"Meditation."

"Okay, how do I meditate? Is there a specific way to sit, any time limit, what object or image do I use?"

"Posture, as far as I am concerned, is not important, except for one key item," I explained, "you can sit like yogis or Buddhists with your legs crossed or you can even stand or lie down. It really does not matter which posture you choose, the key is to keep your spine straight with your neck. You need…"

Meili interrupted by saying, "Why the spine and neck?"

"You need not worry about your legs or arms as long as you are comfortable," I continued, "sorry, I heard you but first I had to complete what I was saying, lest I forgot. Okay, why the spine and neck? Do you know anything about our nervous system?"

"Not much, I'm like, more into math and physics, not anatomy."

"Very well, then, I'll explain," I said, "nervous system is a network of nerves and cells that carry messages to and from the brain and spinal cord to various parts of the body. You see, the brain and spinal cord is the central nervous system, rest of the nerves are branches, like a tree with the central stem with all the branches and sub-branches. Therefore, you want to make sure that all your nerves are active when you meditate. By bending your spine or your neck, you are hindering the transmittal of signals from your brain to other parts of your body, thus the coordination of your actions go out-of-whack, you will not be able to relax all your muscles and will not be able to maintain peace of mind."

"Wow!" Meili exclaimed. "Where did you find that theory, I have never heard or read that before."

"It is not a theory, it is common sense."

"Okay, so what posture is the best?"

"Whichever is easy for you," I said, "I personally prefer laying down on a firm bed with no pillow, so I can fold my legs and have my arms relaxed, that way my spine is straight with my neck."

ShuYa suddenly jumped up, "Is that what you were doing every night when you went to bed, meditating?"

I laughed, so did Meili, then she said to me, "See, your secret is now exposed. So, how long do you meditate?"

"The time frame is not important either," I said, "you can start with as little as 10 minutes a day until you build up the habit. The idea is to learn to focus on one object till you get the hang of it and then you can slowly increase the time of your meditation. Your body and mind gets used to everything, so when you get used to the relaxed position, you can meditate for up to 30 minutes."

"Teach me, how do I start?"

ShuYa was already standing up, she looked at me, and said, "Can we take a tea break before we go into the good stuff?"

"Sure, why not? Let's do that. Do we have any peanuts?"

"I'll make some popcorn."

"What time do we pack in?" I looked at the clock.

"Eleven," ShuYa said as she walked to the kitchen.

"But, Mom, there is no school tomorrow," Meili protested as she looked at me with a sad face, pleading.

"It's okay, we got lots of time," I told her.

After a short break, we gathered back on the couch, except we got ShuYa to sit between Meili and me, so she could hold the bowl of popcorn in her lap. I felt bad to put the burden of popcorn on her but ShuYa was quite happy to please us. What an amazing woman ShuYa was!

"We will start with a few simple questions. I want you to ask yourself—" the professor in me said looking at Meili, "listen carefully and please do not interrupt. Ask yourself, 'Do I want to find myself?' 'Do I have desire, courage, and patience to find myself?' 'Am I a good person?' Remember what is good and what is bad is only an individual's opinion, I have told you my opinion of a good person. 'Am I willing to persist with my search even if I fail a few times?' Remember failure is inevitable, you will fail many times, but you learn with failure. Success eventually comes, as long as you don't quit trying. And finally ask yourself, 'Am I willing to let go my ego, my self-esteem, my pride of my achievement and success?' Did you get all that?" I paused to draw breath, "If you can answer yes to all these questions, you can start meditation."

Meili was busy writing when ShuYa asked her, "Did you get them all?"

"How many questions were there?"

"Six, including the last one."

ShuYa and I waited until Meili finished whatever she was writing. Finally, after a few minutes, she said, "I can answer all those questions. Yes, I am willing to go through all that even if I don't find my soul. What have I got to lose? At worst, I will achieve peace of mind, I will become a good person, and I will develop a concentration tactic which will help me with my studies."

"I am so glad to hear that, I could not have asked for more," I said happily, "under those circumstances, I will teach you how to meditate my way."

"Thank you, I will not disappoint you."

"You are most welcome, my dear, so let's start." I looked at ShuYa, still holding a bowl of popcorn which she offered to me with a smile, "First, find yourself a comfortable position; sitting down, laying down, or standing, no matter which, as long as you are comfortable and can stay in that position for some time. Next, pick an object or anything that you like, something that you can focus on and keep your mind concentrated on it, for example, let's say you pick an apple. Close your eyes and say apple, apple, apple—in your mind quietly. Keep saying apple until it is synchronized with your breathing, which means you breathe in with an apple and you breathe out with an apple. Do that exercise for about ten minutes or until you get tired, no need to refer to clock. Do the same routine for a week or two. By then you will find out if you are comfortable in the posture you have adapted, you will start feeling more relaxed, and your mind will get used to the apple. Then comes the difficult part. This time you can increase your time for meditation. You are now going to start with breathing first. Take a deep breath, hold it for about four seconds, and breathe out. Do this four times, it will help you clear your mind of worldly affairs, then get back to apple." I paused to eat some popcorn. Both girls were silently looking at me with their mouths open. I decided not to speculate on what they were thinking and continued, "After you get back to saying apple, try to visualize an apple in your mind. Focus your mind on an apple, is it green, is it red, what shape is it etc. You will need to do this for as long or as many days as it takes until you can actually see an apple with your eyes closed. This might take weeks or months but do not give up, keep working at it until you find an apple. First, you will see a bright light, as bright as daylight and within that light you will see an apple. Once you find that apple with your eyes closed, you have reached deep inside you and have opened your third eye. Now everything becomes easier, you have developed a tendency to see beyond what your eyes see physically. Keep practicing this tactic for a few more weeks, increasing your time for meditation, then change an object and try with something else, say, an orange. Find out if you can see an orange with your eyes closed."

"You mean I will actually see an apple with my eyes closed?"

"Or any other object that you pick," I said, "try it and you will find out. At least you will develop the power of concentration and will train your mind to focus on a single object. Don't try to rush it or get impatient, sustain your calm, and relax; nothing is easy, nothing is achieved unless you keep plugging at it."

"Wow! That is amazing!" Meili exclaimed, "I want to see things with my eyes closed."

ShuYa laughed, looked at Meili, and said, "All you will see is darkness, at least in the beginning, then who knows?"

"Think positive and put your mind to it," I said, "you can do anything if you keep working at it."

"I think that is too much for one night," ShuYa got up and faced me, "we should stop right here. Give us a chance to digest what you just said and start meditating from scratch."

That night, I kept wondering if what I was teaching Meili was actually right or wrong. Good for one person may not be necessarily good for another. What if something goes wrong? But then, what can go wrong? If she does not like it, she can always drop it and forget about it or she can look elsewhere for a better approach. I finally gave up and went to sleep.

Chapter 7

It was early July, Calgary Stampede was in full swing, some eighteen months after we had had our last discussion. Meili was already eighteen years old, finishing her high school with all A and A+. She got admission in University of Toronto starting September. ShuYa also decided that she would go visit her parents back in China after Meili leaves for Toronto. She, of course, asked me to join her but due to business commitments, I backed out. I was working with my computer on our dining table, posting costs for the project we were doing, our offices were closed for the stampede, ShuYa had gone to work, when Meili came and sat beside me.

"What are you doing?" she asked.

"Posting the cost for the month of June on this project we are working on."

"Would you have some time to talk after you are done with your posting?" she asked politely.

"Sure, any time, this posting can wait," I said, "what do you want to talk about?"

"Me."

"What about you, is something wrong?" I asked, puzzled.

"No, nothing is wrong, on the contrary, everything is good, and that is why I want to tell you about me. I want you to know how I grew up and how I feel today."

"That is very touching, but I think I know who you are. We have been together for the last several years."

"Yes, but now I'll be leaving you for my studies, my mom is also going to China, and you will be all alone."

"Sweetie, I am never alone, God is always with me, and while you are gone, you will still be with me," I said, "besides, we will see you back here during your Christmas break and your mom is only going for two weeks."

"You are so sweet, I love you."

"I love you too." I almost had tears in my eyes. First time in all these years she expressed her feelings towards me, "So, what do you want to tell me about you?"

"Long story, would you like a cup of coffee?"

"I'll get it, you go sit on the couch, and I'll join you there," I said as I closed my laptop and got up. When I got to the living room with a cup of coffee, Meili was on the couch and gestured me to sit beside her.

"I was five years old when my dad disappeared," she began, "I asked my mom where Dad was and all she said was Dad was gone and was never coming back."

"Did he not say anything to you?"

"No, one morning I got up and he was gone. He was always home, did not work, and looked after me. My mom worked at the casino as a dealer full-time and then would study at night, she would prepare meals in the morning before she went to work," Meili said. "My dad would stay home with me and when my mom came home, he would go out."

"That is understandable, somebody had to look after you."

"Yeah, but that was not good enough. I needed somebody to play with or talk to," Meili said sadly. "I always felt so lonely, I didn't have any toys to play with, and all my dad did was sit around and read. My mom brought me some coloring books and that is all I did the whole day, color with crayons and draw. Then one day, Mom got home and was so mad, and then they both started talking loudly in Chinese which I could not understand, and I did not realize that they were fighting because Chinese people always talk so loudly. You see, even today I don't know what happened between them and my mom would not talk about it. You probably know the whole story, I am sure she must have told you."

"No, I don't, because your mom never told me anything. And I never asked."

"Why not?"

"It was in the past and as far as I am concerned, past is dead, you cannot change it nor can you do anything about it. We live in the present and whatever happened in the past is history of our life which we should forget," I said, "anyway, what happened next?"

"After my dad left, he went back to China, and we stayed alone," Meili continued, "my mom would do everything, take me to daycare, go to work, bring me home, feed me, wash me, and play with me or teach me how to draw or read me a story. But something went wrong, I got scared and developed a fear of monsters. I thought a monster took my dad and would someday take my mom away from me too. I was so scared that when we got home,

81

I would not leave my mom alone, always following her everywhere. I had this fear that the monster was hiding in my room and I would close my bedroom door as soon as we got home. Even after I started going to school, the fear of monsters stayed with me, I was always scared of everything and everybody, so I would not talk to anybody, never got associated with any of my school kids except Mary and that only because Mary's dad would pick us up from school and I would stay at their place until my mom came to get me after work. You see, my mom really took good care of me, but I always felt that she was not happy. She had devoted her life to take care of me while sacrificing her own life. She got this accounting job and only worked at the casino on the weekend. In the beginning, I was even scared of Judy, she was my baby-sitter. When my mom went to work at night on the weekend, I would stay awake until Mom got home. Can you imagine what I must have gone through? I don't know how to say it but my whole childhood was a nightmare and then you showed up. First, I thought you were a monster come to take my mom away from me and that scared me even more, I could not sleep at night worrying about Mom but slowly as time went by and you were still hanging around, I saw a difference in my mom, she looked happier and more relaxed," Meili paused while I sat quietly, listening to her story.

"I guess it must be the shock from losing your dad and here I thought you were shy and reserved," I said.

"No, I was scared," Meili continued, "the fear in me was so deep that I didn't know how to get over it. I kept reading books about religion and God, hoping the angel would come one day and take away the monster. Then slowly I noticed how good you were to my mom and me, I started to relax, and when you explained love, I knew that was the answer to my fear—love. Slowly my feelings started to change, fear turned into love and after you explained God, I actually thought God had finally sent an angel to help me."

"Woah, Woah, I am not an angel," I interrupted, "I only brought tim-bits, it was up to you to eat them or throw them away."

"No, you brought love into our life and no matter what you say, to me you will always be an angel," Meili had tears in her eyes, "I will miss you."

"I'll miss you too," I said, controlling my tears, "sweetie, you will always be my daughter."

The door opened and ShuYa walked in, "Who is your daughter?" she asked.

"Meili."

Epilogue

The girls had left, one to China and other to Toronto and I needed a pair of shoes, so Friday evening I went to the mall. After my shopping was done, I went to the food court for a meal.

I was just finishing my supper, when I heard a familiar sweet young girl's voice, "May I sit here?"

I looked up to see a little skinny old lady, with a wrinkled face, short grey hair and piercing eyes smiling at me. Surprised, I said, "Please do, what brings you here?"

"Came to see how you were. How is the girl?"

"She is in Toronto, in the university," I said. "Thank you for saving her life."

"I did not, you did," she smiled. "Calling the ambulance was the right thing to do. If you had taken her to the hospital by yourself with 3-4 hours wait time, she might not have made there in time for the surgery."

"Was she that serious?"

The little lady did not reply, just kept smiling. After a few minutes, she got up and said, "I have to go now, you take care and look after your family. You still have more work to do." She started walking away.

"What!" I exclaimed. "Wait a minute." I was talking to the air, the little old lady was gone. Just then I remembered the note she had left me a few years ago which was still in my wallet. I dug into my wallet and pulled the note out. When I unfolded the piece of paper, I almost fell off my chair. The paper was totally blank.